Annick Press gratefully acknowledges the contribution of
the Canada Council and the Ontario Arts Council,
as well as the Secretary of State.


**Canadian Cataloguing in Publication Data**

Day, Shirley, 1932–
  Ruthie's big tree

(Kids at the corner)
ISBN 0-920236-33-2 (bound).—ISBN 0-920236-35-9 (pbk.)

I. Title.  II. Series.

PS8557.A9R87   jC813'.54   C82-094740-7
PZ7.D39Ru


Distributed in Canada and the USA by:
Firefly Books Ltd.
3520 Pharmacy Avenue, Unit 1-C
Scarborough, Ontario
M1W 2T8


Printed by Johanns Graphics Limited
Waterloo, Ontario

# Ruthie's Big Tree

## by
## Shirley Day

ANNICK PRESS LTD., Toronto, Canada M2M 1K1

Ruthie's best friend in all the world was a weeping willow tree.
This old tree had lived on the vacant lot next door to Ruthie's house
for a very long time. The vacant lot belonged to old man Tester
who didn't know much about children.

Ruthie went every day to climb in the big tree.
She had a secret place to sit
where the leaves hung down
and no one could see her.

She told her secrets to the tree
and the big tree whispered back to Ruthie.

At night, when she was in her bed,
Ruthie could hear the leaves rustling in the wind.
It sounded like the tree was calling her name.

The other children on Ruthie's street
loved that tree too.
When old man Tester was at work
they all came to play with Ruthie
in the tree.

Sometimes the branches
became horses
and the children pretended
they were cowboys
riding on bucking broncos.

At other times the old tree
was a huge space ship
that flew the children
right up to the moon.

Once they were explorers
looking for a new land.
Then the tree was a sailing ship
racing over the waves of grass below.

One day, when Ruthie was sitting alone
on her favourite branch,
old man Tester came out of his house
and marched over to the big tree.
Ruthie was afraid he would see her
but he didn't look up.

He took a hammer out of his pocket
and nailed a sign onto the tree.
After he went back into his house
Ruthie climbed down to see what was on the sign.
It said, **"FOR SALE"**.

Ruthie ran home to tell her mother,
and the next day everyone knew
that the vacant lot with the big tree was for sale!

Many people came to look at the lot but no one bought it.
They said the lot was too small or the tree was too big.
Some said there was not enough sun for a garden.

FOR SALE

Old man Tester was becoming impatient.
So, one morning, before he went to work,
he painted a red **X** on the big tree.
Then he phoned the Tree Service to come and cut it down.

When Ruthie came out to play
she could see that something was wrong.
The big tree looked very sad with that red **X** painted on its trunk.

Rain was falling gently.
The drops fell like tears off the drooping branches.
Ruthie and her friends wondered what was going to happen!

They soon found out when the Tree Service truck stopped
in front of the vacant lot.
Two men jumped out and took a chain-saw from the back of the truck.

Ruthie had never done anything like this before,
but when she saw the tree cutters
with their ropes and saws
she couldn't stand still any longer.

As quick as a cat she dashed over to the big tree
and scampered up to her favourite branch.
"Don't worry," she whispered.
"I won't let them cut you down!"

When the other children saw what she had done
they cheered. "Hurray for Ruthie!" they yelled.

The men stopped work and scratched their heads.
"Hey kid, get out of that tree!" they shouted.

But Ruthie just sat there.

FOR SALE

The men decided to stop for coffee.
They would have to ask their boss what to do.

When her mother came home from work Ruthie was still sitting in the tree.

FOR SALE

A small crowd of people had gathered,
but no one could persuade Ruthie to come down.
Ruthie's mother went into the house to make dinner.
She thought Ruthie would come down when she was hungry.

But Ruthie was determined to stay in that tree all night
if she had to.

The other children began to get hungry now.
They waved good-bye to Ruthie and slowly left the vacant lot.
"We'll be back right after dinner," they promised.


Now Ruthie was all alone.
She was getting a little wet, although the big tree
kept most of the rain from soaking her.

She worried that her friends
wouldn't be allowed out after dinner.
It would be dark and colder pretty soon.
She wondered if she was brave enough to stay there all night.

She might have gone home right then but the Tree Service truck
was still there. She couldn't desert the big tree now.

FOR SALE

After what seemed a long time
Ruthie saw her friend Pete hurrying along the street.
Pete had something for her—
a peanut butter sandwich and two chocolate chip cookies.

Ruthie was glad to see him as he scrambled up the tree.
She was really hungry after all.

The other children started to arrive
and when they saw Ruthie and Pete
both in the tree,
they decided to join them.

One by one they climbed
and soon the big tree
was filled with children.

Just then old man Tester drove up.
He had three people with him—a man, a woman and a small boy.
They all got out of the car and walked over to the big tree.


"What's going on here?" said old man Tester.
"What are all those kids doing in my tree?"
"Why haven't you cut it down?"
The men from the Tree Service started to explain.

Ruthie was frightened when she saw
old man Tester's angry face,
but she just put her arm around a branch
and held on more tightly.
She was glad her friends were with her.

FOR SAL

The people who had come in old man Tester's car
walked over to speak with him.
"But Mr. Tester," said the man,
"you must not cut down this beautiful old tree!
This is just what we have been looking for."

"Yes," said the woman, "children need trees to climb in
and birds need trees to sing in. We want to build our house
right beside this big tree."

The children in the tree cheered loudly.

The little boy said nothing.
He looked at all those children sitting in the tree.
Then he looked at Ruthie.
"This is going to be a good place to live," he thought.


Ruthie climbed slowly down from the tree.
Then she went over to where the boy stood.


"Hello," she said, "I'm Ruthie and this is the big tree.
We're glad you came."
"So am I," said the boy.
"That's the best tree I've ever seen!"

The next day
when the children came to play,
the sign said **"SOLD"**,
and Ruthie was sitting on her favourite branch.